MARION, MISSING

A paranormal mystery novella by

RACHEL CAINE

CHAPTER 1

Since the beginning, it had been VALENTINE & SANDS, PRIVATE INVESTIGATORS. They'd bought furniture in pairs: chairs, bookcases, lamps. One desk, though: a double-sided partner's desk so they had to face each other every day. Hadn't been a chore. They'd liked each other well enough.

Warren Valentine sat in his chair and watched the guy in the white painter's jumpsuit scrape the names off the door. Funny that he was dressed like a painter just to take something off.

"When are you moving out?" the not-painter asked, and took his razor blade to the gold letters of *Private Investigators*. Too bad he didn't scrape the *Investigators* part off first.

"Soon."

"I'm asking 'cause the super said—"

"Soon." Valentine opened a drawer and took out his gun, pulled it out of the holster, and put it on the desktop. In his experience, nothing shut up a talkative busybody faster than that.

Didn't work on this guy, though. "Super said you got shot."

"No."

"Huh. He was pretty sure. Was it your partner?"

Valentine unloaded the .45's clip, snapped the bullet out of the chamber, and caught it in midair. He didn't comment. The not-painter stared at him for a second. Valentine stared back. Then he put the loose bullet in the clip, slipped it back in, and racked the slide.

The guy laughed uncomfortably. It was a whistle-past-the-graveyard kind of laugh. "Right," he said. "You're not talking about it. Got that."

"Glad we have an understanding." Valentine looked at the glass. He could still see a ghost of letters. Maybe it was just his eyes. Maybe it was his imagination. "Make sure you get it all off."

"Sure, sure, boss. Whatever you say." The man had an attitude, even now.

Valentine eyed the gun lying on the green leather inset in the desk, and wondered whether he'd lost his edge, maybe. In the old days nobody would have given him that tone, especially not some guy hired to scrape some paint off a door.

"There. Clean as a whistle."

Valentine studied it. Looked clean from his angle, but when he blinked, he could still see the gold letters. *VALENTINE & SANDS*. Blinked again. Gone.

"Okay," he said. Wouldn't be his problem long anyway. The movers would be coming in to haul off the lamps, the chairs, the file cabinets, the partner desk. All he had to do was dump files in boxes and haul them down to the car. What the hell he'd do with them after that, he didn't know. Maybe pile them up in a hole and burn them, roast a couple of frankfurters and drink a beer like it was a damn picnic.

He didn't really notice when the scraper left, just saw when he looked up again that the door was shut. The blind was drawn on the inside, so he couldn't see whether or not the letters were still there or not. Didn't matter. As long as he couldn't see them.

"Really?" Tilde Sands sounded like she'd found it funny. "That's how you're handling it? Moping like some sad sack whose girl dumped him?"

"You weren't my girl," he said. "And you didn't dumped me. You're still here."

He looked up. She was leaning in the doorway to the file room, a dim silhouette in a pencil skirt and fluffy sweater, heels too high for practicality, her hair down over her shoulders. Sometimes she wore it up, but not today; today it was a dark wave flowing with faint rivers of auburn. Her face was mostly in shadow, but not her pointed chin. Not her mouth, glossy with the reddest lipstick he'd ever seen. Not the warm woody brown of her skin, and the faintly darker mole at the corner of her mouth.

Tilde. Matilde, to everyone but him.

"Val," she said, "you've really got to let go of the past. Now get in here and pull some files. You look like a cliché sitting there. All you need is a half-empty bottle of cheap scotch."

"Be fair," he said. "I like vodka. Doesn't leave a smell that upsets the clients."

"Come get the files."

"Fuck the files," he said, and used his foot to push a chair out on the other side of the partner desk. "Sit your ass down if you're staying. Keep walking if you're not."

"I'm not staying," she said, but she didn't leave either. He knew she was staring at him. He could feel it. "Val—"

"Take a look and see if that idiot left part of the name on the door, would you?"

"You look. You're the one who cares."

He stared at her for a long time, and then got up, jerked the door open, and stared at the glass. He was right. The letters had been there long enough to leave a faint ghost on the surface, readable if you stood at the right angle. Son of a bitch.

When he looked back, Tilde was sitting in the chair on her side of the empty desk with her legs crossed. She'd pulled her hair back, and was winding it up into a bun on the back of her head. A thin yellow pencil secured it in place. He remembered when she'd used nothing but chopsticks, glossy lacquer ones with dangling beads or good luck symbols. These days, a pencil would do. They'd both come down in the world.

"You sticking around, Tilde?"

This was the third time he'd seen her since she'd been found; he'd seen her four times before that. She was still pretty, for the most part; her dark eyes still glimmered under long lashes, her high cheekbones gave her face a lush, heart-shaped look. The only things that gave away the game were the uneven spots on her fluffy white sweater. There hadn't been as much blood as you'd think, for a woman stabbed twelve times with an ice pick.

The first couple had been to the heart, and after that, it was just liquid wicking out. You had to be alive to pump blood out of open wounds.

"I can't stay away," Tilde told him. "The case is still open."

"I'm not working the case."

She said nothing. There was a maddening little smile on those carmine lips, and her sharp, narrow eyebrows canted up. Tilde didn't smoke, but if she did, he thought she'd have been cradling one between her fingers, letting the smoke curl up like a question mark.

For a ghost, she was damn persistent, and the sight of her made him feel sick, weak, and useless.

"Just go," he told her. "I can't help you, doll, and you won't help me. All you gotta do is tell me who did it. That's all."

The silence was as dark as her eyes. He'd asked her that first night, while she was still missing, while she'd sat on the edge of his bed and looked around his cramped little apartment with distaste. He'd thought then that she was really there, really alive, until he'd put his hand right through her. She'd already been dead, wearing that same fuzzy sweater with those uneven bloody polka dots. Her body had been drying out behind the trashcans on Lancaster Street, out back of the massive Deco block of the train station.

She'd been there for three long summer days before somebody found her. Well, the flies had found her. Ants. A stray dog or two. Summer was a hard time to die in Fort Worth, Texas.

Hell and Texas. Hard to tell the two apart, sometimes.

"C'mon, Tilde," he said, even though he knew it wouldn't do any damn good. "Just spill. What's his name? What's he look like? What the hell were you doing out behind the damn train station?"

He didn't know, because they'd had a bust-up over the case she'd been working. When he'd first partnered up with her, he'd hired her on as a secretary. Then she'd brought him a Negro case, but he'd refused to work it. She'd done it instead, and done so damn well she'd presented him with the finished work, case files and all. He'd started using her on other cases, reluctantly. Eventually, somehow, she got to be a partner. After that, he'd made a strict rule: no Negro cases, even though she was one.

She'd glided along with that—or so he'd thought—for about a year, and then she'd told him, flat out, that she earned half the money, and she'd take whatever damn case she wanted, and he could fly a kite. Tilde could be hard like that, though she looked soft as a kitten. Turned out she'd been taking cases from her people the whole time, off the books, getting paid in cash. She'd thrown a couple thousand bucks his way when he yelled about it.

"There's your cut!" she'd said, and that had stunned him into silence. That, and picking up the bills.

But he hadn't wanted her looking into *this* case. Not this one. She'd been the first to see there was some kind of pattern... women around her own age, Negroes and a couple of Latinas, disappearing. Not from their houses or cramped apartments, but from the street, where they were out shopping or drinking or dancing. Went out, never went home.

Oh, they were found. Eventually. First one had been rolled down a levee of the Trinity River. Second one into a gully in the trash-tree no-man's-land outside of downtown Fort Worth. Third left in a park, by a stream.

Things had been done to them that looked awful similar— strangled, raped, icepicked. She'd found more of them, searching the police records—four more. Some had been drunks, some prostitutes, some homeless wandering the street. All dead, stripped, left like bags of trash in parks, ditches or gullies. Always near water.

Police had arrested three men for three of the murders— husband, boyfriend, pimp. Cops hadn't looked bothered to get creative. Hell, Val didn't even blame them, those were the odds-on favorites for any woman's death. Somebody she knew, somebody she loved, somebody she worked for, or with.

It had been a dog loser of a case, and he'd told Tilde so,

straight up. She'd yelled right back at him to drop dead.

Drop dead.

Sickly funny when he thought about it.

"So you're quitting," Tilde told him. "Giving up. Why, Val? You're a good man. You do good work."

"If you call snapping pictures of cheating wives and husbands for divorce court good, sure."

"That's not all you do. You've helped people."

He had no argument for that. There'd been plenty of desperate people who'd come in that door, and he and Tilde had found ways to make things better for most. Half them came looking or family members who'd disappeared. Often he and Tilde had found their loved ones alive, sodden drunk or hyped out of their minds, or just plain sick of home.

Other times they found them in the morgue, but at least the families knew. That was something.

"Val, this wasn't your fault," Tilde said, and picked at one of the dried red dots on her sweater. Not really dots, he decided. More like lopsided bloody flowers. "None of it was your fault."

"You went out there alone while I was off doing some damn stupid thing or other. Don't sell me shit and call it sunshine."

She smiled. He remembered that smile so well. Pretty girl, Tilde; self-contained and self-reliant, too. She'd made it clear from the time she'd presented her P.I. license that she wasn't going to be his secretary any more, and she wasn't going to be his chippie or his piece on the side. She was a detective. She was going to be treated like one.

And though he knew it wasn't smart, he'd fallen half in love with her right then.

"Language," she said, and it was half a purr, teasing and sweet. Just the way she'd have said it on a day when she was still living, when their names were still on the door.

"I saw you on the slab. Don't give me shit about my

language." Funny, the coroner's office was the one place in town where white and colored folk mixed together in harmony—the dead didn't care. Of course, they didn't let the white families back there where all the races mingled. They showed them their dead in a special viewing room. But he'd seen *her* on a cold table in the middle of a rainbow of skin tones, and she'd been the darkest of all of them.

She hadn't been the prettiest, not anymore. He'd never puked his guts up before at the morgue, not ever, but that day ... that day he'd puked and cried and put his head in his hands like any other damn fool who'd never faced death straight on. Stupid. He'd been to war, he'd seen things.

He hadn't seen a woman he loved reduced to decaying raw meat before.

"Focus," she said, and he snapped out of the memory and into the present like she'd put a cold hand on his forehead. She hadn't. She was still sitting cross-legged in the wheeled wooden chair on the other side of the desk.

It usually creaked when she leaned forward, but it didn't now. *Because she's not really here,* he told himself. *Because you've cracked like an egg, buddy. The diner down the block could make an omelet out of you.*

"You need to get back to work. You're good at this. You make the world better when other people tear it down. I need you to keep doing that."

"What are you, my mother?"

"No," Tilde said, and tilted her head to one side. It revealed one last wound, the one on the side of her head, right in the temple, where she'd been icepicked in the brain just to be sure. A little trickle of red down the side of her face, bright as her lipstick, and the wounds in her chest took on brighter centers. "I have to go now," she told him. "Listen to your partner. Don't quit on me. Don't you *dare*."

She smiled, and it was the sweetest thing. Made him think of sunrises and hope.

Then the partner chair sat empty, and except for a lingering whisper of that perfume she always wore, Tilde was gone again.

"God damn you," he whispered, and clutched the edge of the desk in shaking hands. "God damn you for leaving."

CHAPTER 2

He was putting the last of the files into boxes—haphazard piles, nothing like *she* would have done because Tilde had always been a stickler for having everything done just so—when a knock came on the door. Probably the super coming to tell him to finish up, or the painter coming to put somebody else's name on the door, painting a shiny new one over the ghost of VALENTINE & SANDS. They didn't let grass grow under empty listings.

But it was a pair standing there, man and woman with graying hair and sagging, defeated faces, and he knew exactly what they wanted. He'd become an expert in fear. A goddamn genius at grief. The woman was short, dowdy, wearing a shapeless coat that wouldn't have done a Hollywood starlet any favors, much less a Southern housewife. She had on painfully clean white cotton gloves, and a hat that looked like her best, and shoes with a one-inch heel and wide toes. Support hose.

The man was taller, thinner, almost hidden in his black suit. He'd lost weight recently, and the suit hung on him like a costume on a scarecrow. He needed a cut and a shave, and unlike his wife's hat, his fedora had seen better days. Maybe a better decade.

They were Negroes. And Val knew right off they weren't here for him. "Sorry," he said. "She's gone."

"Yes sir, we know all about Matilde," the man said, and quickly doffed his hat. He turned it in his hands, round and round, "You're Mr. Valentine?"

"I'm just here to clean out the office." That made it sound like he was some hired hand. He hoped that would do the job.

"But you *are* Warren Valentine," the woman said. "She

talked about you. Said you were the best, sir."

He avoided the wife's eyes. The women always got to him, especially the mothers, with their desperate hope and tears they tried not to shed. The men were easier. They only let the grief out in nervous gestures, like the way the man in front of him handled that hat.

They already knew who he was, so he faced them head on. "You were acquainted with Miss Sands?"

"She was our niece," the man said.

Maybe this was some misplaced condolence call. Did the woman have a covered dish under that shapeless coat?

"She was great," he said. "Look, I wasn't kidding, I'm closing up. Just leaving."

"But you're still working, aren't you, sir? Still taking cases?"

"Not anymore." *Not since Tilde.*

"But—"

"Time to do something else," he said, as if he was kicking dust off his shoes and moving to greener pastures, and that was disrespectful, he knew it as soon as he'd said it.

"Something else?" The woman's question was sharp, and he looked right at her, and there were no tears in her eyes, no desperate shimmers of hope. Valentine wasn't a life preserver in her ocean, he realized. He was a ship she intended to board and commandeer. "You can't do that. You're the best. Matilde said so."

"No offense, ma'am, but Tilde was wrong," he said. "And I'm still closed. Sorry. I wish I could help with whatever—'"

She opened her handbag, took out a photo and held it out. She didn't hand it over, she brandished it like a weapon at him. "This is Marion," she said. "Our granddaughter, Matilde's kin. She's missing. She's been missing days now. We need you to find her."

He tried not to look, but she thrust the picture closer, and there it was. A little girl, maybe eight years old, with springy dark locks and a heartbreaker's smile. The black-and-white photo muddied her features a little, but he recognized the shape of her eyes, the high cheekbones. Family resemblance.

Even the smile was an echo.

"Marion," she said again, firmly. "Matilde would want you to do this, sir. She really would."

Of course she would. Tilde had been here, saying almost the same things to him, half an hour back. She hadn't just gone away, like any decent murder victim; she'd come back to sit on his bed and at their desk, to smile and evade his questions and tell him to get on with it, do what he was supposed to do.

God damn you, girl, he thought, but he couldn't say it out loud to her people. Instead he said, bluntly, "I'm a white man. You really think folk are going to talk to me like they would to her?"

"I think they will, for Matilde," the woman said. After a hesitation, she said, "Are you going to have us in? Or do we have to sit down right here in the hall?"

Val sighed, stepped back, and swung the door open to let them walk inside. He sat on one side of the partner desk, and for a second he was afraid Tilde would be sitting across from him, and they'd *have* to see her, wouldn't they, but she wasn't there. The old man pulled up two plain wooden chairs and helped his wife into one with old-time grace before taking the other for himself.

Val reached out to take the photo of Marion from her grandmother, and said, "Tell me everything."

Marion, Missing

CHAPTER 3

Everything wasn't much. It made one page on a pad of lined paper, in big, sloppy writing, and when the two across from him stopped talking, Valentine tapped the pencil on the pad and considered. Marion Carlyle, eight years old. Playing outside in her fenced yard in the Como section of Fort Worth, east of downtown.

He'd written down the address, but he knew what he was bound to find: a street of neat, cheap little row houses, some kept painfully nice by hardworking people like Grandpa Carlyle and others going to weeds and dirt, peeling paint and sagging fences. Hopeless houses. He wondered which he'd find for Marion.

Marion's father worked at the TESCO plant, just a regular working stiff according to Grandpa, though—and it was a telling admission from family—maybe a little too fond of the bottle. Marion's mother was a homemaker, and by all accounts, little Marion was the light of her life. She'd have come herself, Grandma Carlyle said, but she'd been eaten up with grief.

No word on why Marion's father hadn't come, but Val could guess. The man was finding either solace or forgiveness at the nearest bar that'd serve Negroes.

Marion had been a bright, pretty, neat little girl who liked to read and sing. Nothing special about her, really. Just a girl, smart for her age, who'd been a little shy around those she didn't know. Not outgoing enough to run off with friends on impulse, or take candy from a stranger. A neighbor had heard a cry, and a struggle. She saw somebody pulling the girl into a black car. She hadn't been sure, but she thought the girl's arm might have hung funny.

Broken, maybe.

The cops hadn't done much. Depending on the detective

who'd caught the squeal, that might not have been his fault. Sometimes it was just that white cops didn't get anywhere talking to the Negro neighborhoods, no matter what the cause. And some of the cops didn't much care, either. He'd heard them before, talking about *real* cases, *real* victims. They'd spout some bullshit about how it was probably some relative, or the neighbor had made it all up and the kid was a runaway.

Turned his stomach, then and now. That was part of the reason when Tilde Sands had shown up with her P.I. license and calm, steely attitude he'd decided there was a gain to be made there.

Then and now, maybe.

"Well?" Grandma Carlyle asked him. "We can pay. I'm not expecting no work for free, even though she's just a baby. Even though she's family to Matilde. We can pay—"

"A hundred dollars," Grandpa Carlyle cut in decisively, and reached into his inside coat pocket. He had a flat wallet there, with bills pressed neatly together. Twenties. Five of them.

It was all there was, in the wallet. Val caught the pinched, hunted look Grandma Carlyle had on her face, until she hardened it into a blank mask.

"Tell you what," he said. "I can't give you any guarantees I can make much progress. I'll take twenty as a retainer. We'll settle up once I report back."

"We don't want no favors, young man," Carlyle said. He looked like what he was—an upright, dignified man in the last quarter of his life. A man who'd probably never taken a dime he didn't earn by the sweat of his brow. A man who'd never bought on credit. A church-goer who voted in every election, faithfully, even when others lost that faith.

Val looked at pulling a voting booth lever like playing a broken slot machine. But he wasn't Carlyle. Not even close.

"It isn't a favor," he said. "I work for a living. Tilde would have told you that."

Carlyle frowned, but he nodded and passed over the bill. Val wrote him out a receipt on a corner of his notepad, tore it off, and passed it over. "Sorry. All the receipt pads are packed up."

"This'll do, sir. We trust you."

Carlyle stood up. Mrs. Carlyle—he'd never heard either of their first names, and likely they hardly ever used them anyway—stayed seated with her knees primly together, and her purse on her lap like a dog that might run away. She stared right at Val's face and said, "You believe in spirits, Mr. Valentine?"

"No."

Tilde's whispering laugh came to him from the file room. "Liar." He knew they hadn't heard her.

"I believe," she said. "I believe my niece wants you to find our little Marion. You find that girl. For Tilde."

He stood up and offered his hand to her. He meant to help her up, but she shook it, firm as a man, before she got up all on her own, took her husband's arm, and walked out.

The door closed softly behind them, and the closed blinds swayed. He went and locked it, after. No sense letting more trouble come in.

Barn door, and the horse already bolted, he thought, and before he could turn, he knew Tilde was there. He smelled that light, floral perfume again.

This time, he felt a cold hand stroke gently over the back of his neck. He didn't turn. He was afraid that if he did, he might see the wrong Tilde. The one from his nightmares.

"Thanks," she whispered in his ear, and then she was gone.

Marion, Missing

CHAPTER 4

Driving down Lancaster and into the south side of town meant passing the train station. He didn't like that, didn't like so much as glancing at the block-long, six-story Deco dinosaur that was rapidly losing its luster amid newer, trendier construction.

Trains were starting to lose out to the open road and V8 power, and people traveling on their own on the new highway system. Only a matter of time, he thought, before the old dinosaur ended up tar soup, knocked down for some plain brick row of buildings.

He didn't want to see that happen, but it'd be nice knock it down for other reasons. Tilde's blood had soaked into that ground. Right around the back, by the trash heaps. Maybe that made it worse, that her killer had left her with the garbage.

Not in a park. Not by a river, or even in a gully or a ditch. Those other gals had been found nude. They'd been violated and stabbed and strangled with a man's strong hands before being stabbed. This had been more efficient. Tilde hadn't been raped or mutilated. She'd been fully clothed, killed and left where she dropped.

It didn't sound like the killer she'd been chasing, but what did he know? Ice-cold killers didn't make much sense to him. Heat of passion, robbery, even rape—those he could get his head wrapped around. Those were basic human needs twisted up and made wrong. The cold ones, the ones that seemed like some monster's work... those, he just didn't understand.

He guessed he was glad.

It was still hot. Early September had a special kind of sizzle to it in central Texas; a stillness without breezes, and a merciless sun in a whitened sky. Birds stayed mostly silent, but a chorus of desperate grasshoppers and cicadas came out to whine.

Not the blistering heat of August, but plenty bad enough to

make a man sweat through a couple of shirts a day. This town kept laundries and icehouses in business. *If I owned Hell and Texas, I'd live in Hell and rent out Texas.* General Sheridan had said that. He was a smart man.

It was almost like crossing a border, an invisible line in the sand, between the white part of town and the east-side Negro districts. Almost instantly, the shop windows advertising French fashions and fancy salons disappeared, replaced by dress shops and hair parlors that couldn't afford to charge a tenth of what they did two blocks down. Restaurants served a different menu. And every face he saw on the street was a shade of brown, from tan to mahogany and almost into ebony.

But it was also just the same. Women wore neat dresses that belled out like pastel flowers, and pushed baby carriages just like on the white end of town. Grandmothers carried shopping bags. What seemed different were the hard-eyed young men gathered in threes and fours near the liquor stores, studying his car with blank, angry eyes, though he knew some poor white neighborhoods where he'd get the same. It was just more obvious here.

Val took three turns and found the street he'd scratched out on the pad, and slowed as he looked for house numbers. The one he was looking for was in transition ... it had been trying, not so long ago, for respectability, but was slowly sliding into something like decay. A year too long on the paint. Yard patchy and thinning. One of the windowpanes had cracked right across, and from the dirt on the outside it wasn't a recent event. The house was maybe a year away from dirt, weeds, and cardboard over a hole.

There was a little girl's bicycle leaning up against the house, faded pink handles and ribbons fluttering more from the shimmer of heat than any wind.

Val parked the car and stared out at the house for a minute, taking it in. It was the end of the block, at a cross street, which made it easy for someone to park, grab the kid, and be off again quick. There was a main drag two blocks down. Easy escape. *She could still be alive.*

He didn't believe that much. Rich kids got kidnapped and ransomed back, but poor kids ...poor kids got used up.

"She's strong," Tilde said from beside him. "She's a fighter. Like me. I saw a lot of myself in Marion."

"Is she dead?"

"You tell me." He turned his head and there she was, sitting on the front seat right next to him. From this angle, he couldn't see the wound in her temple, and the mess on her sweater could have just been one of those sloppy modern art designs.

It was hot enough to make the hard plastic steering wheel into a branding iron, but she brought a cool breeze with her. Something eerie about it. Made him shiver. The sunlight wasn't as kind to her as the dim office had been. There was an ashen, silvery cast to her skin, where it had been a warm brown, and a strange, unsettling look in her eyes. The lipstick seemed too wet.

"Hell, I guess we'll play hot and cold, then. Was it someone in the family?"

"No."

"Someone she knew?"

"No."

"A stranger."

No answer. Tilde stared at him—through him, really—in a way that made the hot day seem far away.

"All right. A stranger. On foot?"

"No."

"Car." More silence. He scribbled on his pad, aware he was probably going totally goddamn nuts, because he was asking questions to an imaginary dead partner and pretending like it was solid investigation. "From the neighborhood?"

"No."

"From the city?"

She looked like she thought about it, and then, oddly, shook her head. Halfway between a yes and no, he guessed, so he said, "Near the city?"

Nothing. So, a yes on that point. Not in Fort Worth, but in an area close by. He worked through the cities that bordered, starting with the obvious, Dallas. That was a solid *no.* So were all the other little communities he ran through, until he got to one that bordered Fort Worth to the east, sitting in the open space between Fort Worth and Dallas. "Arlington."

The silence made his skin prickle, like ice had formed. He swore he could almost see his breath on the still air, which was nuts because he was still sweating. He wrote down *Arlington.* Good. Not that big a place. Kind of a backwater, less than ten thousand souls crouched on the prairie between two bigger cities.

"Okay, let's start with the guy—" When he turned his head, she was gone, and the heat smacked him in the face like a hot skillet. He rolled down the window all the way, gasping for air. It must have gotten up to a hundred and twenty inside the car, and he hadn't felt it until that second.

Val swallowed back the taste of steaming hot metal and dry, burned grass, and got out of his car to walk to the house where Marion lived.

Or at least, he hoped she still did.

CHAPTER 5

"Y'all be some kind of crazy," said Marion's father. He was drunk off his ass and sitting in a chair that had seen better days during the Hoover administration. "You take money off my pops to ask *me* shit? Wouldn't be sitting here if I knew where she was. I ain't no coward."

Not much of a father, either, Val thought. The man was a strange mix of young and old, sitting in his creaky armchair and cradling a bottle of what looked like no-name whiskey. The house smelled of unemptied trash and neglect, but he had the feeling that was a recent enough development. "Maybe I can talk to your wife," Val said. "Seeing as how your parents sent me here."

"Doc gave her some sleeping pills. She ain't hardly been up for days. Why the place is such a mess." Mr. Carlyle the younger, Val thought, wasn't making this easy for him, but he intended to try. There was a girl out there who needed to come home. Dead or alive.

And there was Tilde.

"Where was Marion last seen?"

"In the yard, 'bout four o'clock. 'Round six we were setting for dinner and the neighbor came over yelling somebody had grabbed our little girl. I called the police. They rolled up the next morning."

For a moment, Mr. Carlyle Junior seemed to come out of his alcoholic stupor, and there was a moment of realization on his face. Must have been real bitter.

"They had their coffee with 'em. Drinking coffee while they sat here and told me and my wife our little gal musta just wandered off. The neighbor wasn't what they called *credible*. Asked if we beat Marion. Hell no, I don't beat that girl! Marion's a good girl." He stared off into the distance for a few seconds, then said, in a softer voice, "Always been a good girl. Smart, too. Liked to keep her clothes all neat; not a tomboy like some. Just a pretty little girl. God almighty."

"What was she wearing?"

"Pink dress," Carlyle said in the same soft tone. "Pink like those flowers we get 'round here in the spring, you know, the weedy ones. Pale pink. She had on white ankle socks and black shoes. And she had her hair done up in pigtails. Little pink ribbon bows."

"Sounds like she was heading out somewhere, not just out playing."

"She was going to church after dinner with my wife. Got all pretty for it."

"You don't go with them?"

"Naw." His pew was the barstool; that was clear enough from the look Carlyle gave the bottle. He took another sip. "Didn't remember that before, about her clothes. See it clear as day now, like she was standing there. Right there, in the door." He was staring at the front door. "You believe in ghosts, Mr. Valentine?"

"No," he said.

"Liar," Tilde breathed, right behind his ear, and he flinched. When he looked at the front door, he saw her leaning there, arms crossed. Smiling that red, wet smile.

"I don't," he said, and turned back to Carlyle. "She might still be alive."

Carlyle just shook his head and took another long pull on the bottle. Didn't say another word, no matter what Valentine asked. Maybe he *had* seen his little girl. Maybe there was nothing more to say.

Valentine passed over his business card and asked him to have his wife call when she felt up to it, and left.

CHAPTER 6

The maybe-broken-arm was a good place to start, because after talking to the neighbor, Val discovered she was a local midwife; she knew enough medicine to know a broken arm when she saw one. The little girl had yelled, too.

So maybe, just maybe, a kidnapper would have gotten the arm seen to, if only to stop her crying.

Val made the usual rounds of the Fort Worth clinics and hospitals that took Negro patients. The regular Negro hospital, Ethel Ransom, had closed last year, so that meant visiting the basement of St. Joseph's, with no luck. That left him with four clinics, and probably about fifty quacks who dispensed fixes on the sly at ten times the price. He didn't bother making the rounds to the quacks. They weren't going to admit anything, especially if the girl had been brought in.

Once he'd used up the leads for his own town, he decided to make the fifteen mile drive to Arlington, past some rolling hills and areas thick with trash trees and brush. The place was growing, and someday it'd shape up to be a real town, but not yet.

He didn't know the burg quite as well as he ought to, and stopped off at a diner to consult a phone book. There was only one clinic in Arlington that said NEGROES WELCOME.

The place sat near the edge of town on the southeastern side, away from anything that might have been remotely scenic. It was just flat land, scrub, and weeds, with buildings struggling up in the middle.

Harry Truman had rolled through this no-horse town not so long ago, waving and smiling at the crowds lining Main Street, but Arlington wasn't much. Black folks—if they lived here—had to go as far as the next town over for a diner meal, much less medical care, except for this one sad little building. Arlington was a profoundly white town.

Val walked into the clinic and ten pairs of eyes immediately locked on him—nine dark-skinned patients, and a white nurse. She was impeccable in a crisp white cap and uniform, but she had a flat, suspicious stare.

Val crossed to the window at the counter. "Howdy," he said, and tipped his hat politely. She gazed at him without blinking. "Looking to see if you might have maybe treated this little girl here in the last few days."

He handed over the photo. Behind him, he heard people quietly getting up, and the door opening and closing. The nurse looked irritated, and took the picture to give it a scan so fast he was sure she couldn't have recognized it from a bull moose.

"No," she said, and thrust it back. "Please go. You're disturbing our patients."

It sounded like *patience,* and she probably meant it either way. "Yeah, well, sorry, but you're going to have to take another look."

"Please leave."

He leaned forward. Under the suit jacket, the shoulder holster was totally visible, with the butt of the .45 aiming straight at her.

"Look," Val said. "I'm not here to blow whatever deals you've got going on, sister. I just want to know if you've seen this girl. I'm working for her family. She got snatched."

He slid the photo over again, and after a hesitation, the nurse took it, gave it a good stare, and handed it back. She wasn't glaring at him now. She was looking down. "No," she said. "I'm sorry. She hasn't been here."

He felt the cold touch on the back of his neck. *Tilde.* Maybe she wasn't there at all, maybe it was just his instincts yelling, but he didn't care. Worked the same way.

Because the nurse was lying her lips off.

"Mind if I talk to the doctor?" he asked her, and kept it all sugar sweet and butter wouldn't melt.

"Got a badge?"

He showed his P.I. license without comment. In his experience, most people didn't know the difference anyway; it was all in the attitude. She hadn't asked if he was a cop, and he hadn't lied.

She walked back down a narrow, dark hallway to an office at the back.

Nicer than he expected. There was a doctor in a white coat behind a desk. He was an older man, white, with a gleaming smile that Val immediately disliked. What was a white doc doing over here tending to Negro folks when he could be raking it in on the other side of town? Chances were, he'd been drummed out of the hospitals or sued for malpractice, or was known for drinking his lunch at the nearest watering hole. Lushes made bad doctors, and this one had the red nose and watery eyes of dedicated boozer. His breath smelled like medicine, like he'd just gargled out the whiskey.

"Help you, detective?" he asked, and there it was, a very slight slur in the words. Val resisted the urge to grab the man by his thin necktie and slam his face into the desk.

"Yeah," he said, and slapped down the picture of Marion. "I'm looking for this kid. Was she here?"

The doctor focused bleary eyes, pursed his lips, and sobered up real quick. He didn't want Val to see it, but Val saw it anyway—along with the way his body leaned away from the desk, like wanting to get the hell away from that picture without being too obvious about it. He was a better liar than his nurse; he studied the photo for a long moment before handing it back with a brisk, "No, never seen the girl. Is she in some trouble?"

"Bank robber," Val said. Most people would have laughed. The doc just looked confused, like he'd had his reply all ready and Val's had derailed it with a crash. "When was she here?"

"I said—"

Val walked to the desk, put his palms on it, and leaned. Up

close, the doc's eyes were a Rorschach test of fine little threads of red; and though his breath smelled of Listerine, his body sweated pure alcohol. "Don't bullshit me, doc. When?"

"I can't—"

"*When*?" Val's voice came out a roar this time, loud enough to part the man's hair, and when the doctor tried to wheel his chair backward, Val grabbed him by that skinny tie and held him in place. "God damn you, you're going to answer me, you low-life drunk!"

"Rollins!" the doc yelped, still frantically trying to roll himself back and away from Val. The effect was getting him nowhere. "It was Rollins who brought her in. I had nothing to do with it, I swear! Look, I did my best, okay? She left here alive!"

"How much alive?" The doc's mouth moved, but he didn't answer. His face was getting purple, and Val realized he'd been racking that tie tighter, tighter, and twisting it as he listened. For a black moment he thought, *well, what the hell, who's going to kick about it,* but then he loosened his grip and let the clown gasp for air.

He repeated the question. "How much alive was she?"

"Drugged, but breathing," the doctor said in a husky, bruised voice. "You want Rollins, not me. Chess Rollins. He's the one who dragged her in here."

Val didn't really want to know, but he had to ask. "What was wrong with her?"

"Fell and broke her arm."

Sure. Sure, she had. "What else?" The doc's gaze slid away from his like eggs on a greasy plate, and he rattled him good to get him focused. "*What else*?"

"He'd given her something. She was half out of it. Look, detective, Rollins said she was his own kid. How was I to know—"

Val shoved him back in the chair hard enough that it rolled away from the desk and hit the wall behind with a dull *thump* and nearly tipped right over. The doc struggled for balance, still red in the face and breathing hard. He looked scared, which was good. Val didn't dare let him have time to slide from scared to angry. "Rollins. Where can I find him?"

"He didn't interfere with the girl none that I could see—" Not, Val thought, that he'd bothered to check. The doc gulped at the look in his eyes. "Shack out on the far south side, 'round Pleasant Ridge Road out in those trees. Just ask anybody 'round there, they all know him. But you'd better go loaded for bear. Tough customers out that way."

Val took out his .45 and shoved it right into the doc's chest. "Tough customers all over, buddy. You close up shop."

"For how long?"

"Until I say different."

The doctor made one last try to grab his dignity back. He straightened his tie and coat and cleared his throat and tried to sound sober as a judge. "See here, I am a *doctor,* and my patients are in need of—"

"Your patients need a doc that doesn't drink three meals a day," Val finished for him. "And somebody that doesn't give out aspirin for cancer, and charge like it's a gold plated fucking miracle."

"They take what they can get!" The doc was getting mulish now. "Without me, half of them would be seeing some witch doctor with a bone through his nose!"

Val stared at him. He still had a .45 to the man's chest, and the urge to pull was damn near irresistible, but instead he whipped the barrel around and cracked the doc on the side of the head. Not enough to break his skull, just enough to leave a dent and one hell of a headache.

"If I find out you could have saved this girl and you didn't, I'll come back," he said. "It'd be a damn sight better for you if I find this place locked up and you gone off retired. Understand?"

The doc held his bloody head, cringed, and nodded. He looked scared enough to piss his pants, which was exactly what

Val wanted.

"If you call this Rollins and warn him I'm coming, retirement won't save you. Florida, Bora Bora, doesn't matter. I'll find you."

"I won't call," the doc whimpered. "Jesus. *Jesus.* What's wrong with you, you animal?"

"You'd better hope like hell you never find out."

The nurse was hovering outside the office, but she yelped and ran off when he came out, gun still in his hand. He wiped the blood off the gun on a piece of gauze and walked out of the now-empty waiting room. The doc *might* get the wild notion to call the cops, but Val couldn't see it. They'd ask too many questions. Cockroaches like him didn't like the light.

Tilde leaned against the front fender of the car. Her white sweater was damp with blood again, red floral centers to the stab wounds. The one in her head was trickling a little stream down the line of her chin. "Find something?" she asked him.

He ignored her and walked to the driver's side, got in, and rattled the old Chrysler to life. The bodywork was junk, but the engine had a heart of V8 gold. Tilde appeared on the passenger seat when he put the car in gear. He could see her out of the corner of his eye. "Do you know where you're going?"

"To see this Rollins."

"Val." Against his will, he looked at her, and she was smiling. He knew that smile. It broke his heart. "You can't save me, but you can still save Marion. I need you to do that. For me."

The fingers of her left hand stroked his right where it gripped the red-hot steering wheel, and the burning sensation from the Bakelite vanished. He lost the feeling in his fingertips, and they looked pale.

"Promise me you'll do that," she said.

He yanked his attention back to the road. He was sitting in the parking lot entrance, idling, when there was a whole empty street ahead of him.

He cranked the wheel to put the car onto Tom Lee Road. He was already pretty far south, but he had to go farther, to the very backwater edges, where tarpaper shacks with no connection to electric or running water still lurked. Rollins hadn't built it ... his type never built anything. Squatter, most likely.

It was a hell of a place to bring a child.

His stomach was felt hollow. He wasn't hungry, he still wished he'd eaten something to fill that hole, make him feel stronger.

The clapboard houses of Arlington fell away into open fields reaping nothing but dry stalks; the heat had burned off most of the cash crops this year, and some of the farms he drove past were already abandoned. More would go next year. There was talk the new town mayor had ambitious plans for the place, getting industry and tourism, but out here it was just poverty and despair, and not much hope for the future.

It was even farther out to Pleasant Ridge Road—the far side of nowhere. Couldn't even see civilization from out here, just trees and weeds and trotting across the road like it hadn't a care in the world, a lone coyote. The road was more of a suggestion of one, and like to break an axle if Val tried to go faster than a crawl.

But somebody had been on it enough to groove fresh tracks. He watched those tracks, and saw where they turned off on an overgrown path into a stand of trees. No sense being stupid about it. Val pulled his car off to the side, parked, and went on foot.

The heat felt like a hand crushing around him, and before he'd gone ten feet from the car he'd already sweated through his shirt, again. He pulled the gun from his holster and held it ready as he walked up the path, listening to singing crickets and droning cicadas, and the strange, distant sound of someone singing.

Twenty feet on, he recognized it for a record playing, some torch singer from the '40s who had a low, throaty voice that reminded him of gin and velvet. The music was coming from a one-room shack with a roof that dipped drunkenly in the middle—scrap wood and tarpaper, not even a proper cabin. A good straight-line wind would take it down. It was almost invisible in the shadow of the live oaks towering above it.

He heard the *snick* of a gun being cocked, and threw himself behind the thick trunk of a tree just before he heard the boom. Sounded like a .38 to him, and he risked a look around the tree to see the snub-nosed chrome barrel pointing out of the shack's open window. Light flared, and he ducked back. The shot missed even the tree. "You get on outta here!" A man's voice from the shack, thick and angry. "I'll kill ya!"

I can't shoot direct, he thought. The .45's slugs would tear right through one side of that place and out the other, and if Marion Carlyle was in there, he couldn't risk hitting her. Instead, he placed a shot well above the top of the window. It blew a nice-sized hole in the thin wood.

The other man squawked and the gun pulled back. "Look," Val said, in what he hoped was a reasonable tone. "You got me all wrong, pal. Let's not stage World War Three out here; we just finished up the last one. I just wanted to ask you a question, that's all."

There was a short delay. The man inside shuffled around, and the music cut off with a scratch. "What kinda question?"

"How about I come in and ask? I'm getting bit all to hell out here by these skeeters. Couple of wasps' nest out here, too. Not fond of 'em."

"Me neither," the man said. More shuffling. "All right. You come on."

"Don't you try to shoot me, son. This cannon doesn't have to be half accurate to blow you in two."

"Yeah, I know it. Come on."

Val didn't trust him, but the sweat on his face attracted mosquitos that danced in a cloud around his face, and he smashed at them irritably and looked at the smear of blood left on his hand. He kept the gun ready as he walked toward the shack, the whine of buzzing bugs heavy in his ears, and then he saw Tilde.

Nightmare Tilde.

She was lying on the ground in the shack's shadow, thrown there like an empty sack. Her eyes were dull, her white shirt stained with blood that had gone black and hard. Her cheeks were sunken, and flies crawled over her. Over her open eyes.

He sucked in a gasp and stopped, and *blink*, she was gone. Instead, Tilde was standing right in front of him, looking almost perfect in these shifting leafy shadows. She said, "Don't you trust him, Val. Not for a second."

He didn't. He nodded to her and walked on, and the door of the shack yawned in on darkness. "You throw that cannon down, mister," the man inside said. The man he couldn't see.

"You first."

Something hit the wood floor. Might have been a gun. Might have been a rock. Hard to tell. Val decided not to risk it, and hit the door hard with his shoulder, hard enough to the send the man inside flying back to wham against the far wall, where he tripped over a filthy camp bed and fell on it so hard the canvas tore and dumped him through the frame.

Rollins was still holding the .38, but Val had him dead to rights, he knew it. He dropped the gun and held up his hands.

The inside of the cabin was worse than the outside, filled with trash and old bottles. Nothing worthwhile but a gas camp stove, old Victrola, bed, and filthy blanket.

There was no sign of Marion.

"What you want, mister?" Rollins was a white man, hillbilly thin, with faded brown hair that rose high up on his forehead and watery light-colored eyes. Rotten teeth, what ones he had. The reek of him was like an animal kept in too small a cage. "I ain't done nothing!"

"Little girl," he said, and took the picture out of his pocket. "You know where she is. Now you're going to tell me."

Rollins looked at the kid, and his mouth fell open to give Val a complete view of the extent of the tooth rot. "Don't know nothing!" he yelped, and tried to scramble up.

Val stepped forward and kicked the .38 away into the shadows, where it knocked over a pyramid of beer bottles, and pressed the muzzle of the .45 to Rollins's forehead. Not exactly a small target.

"Then it doesn't matter if I kill you or not," he said. "Unless you do know something. In which case I might not pull this trigger."

Rollins went the shade of bad milk, and his eyes filled with tears. Val smelled urine, and didn't need to look down to know how scared the man was.

"Please," he said. "Please, mister; ain't none of my doing, I got nothing to do with any of it. I just took some money, that's all! Just a little money, to watch her until they came back! And—" His eyes flickered, like a film stuttered behind them. "And her arm was broke and I got it fixed and all. I helped her!"

"Yeah, you're a real hero, pal. Who brought her here?"

"What?"

"You heard me."

"Mister—" Rollins licked his lips. "A'right. It was Captain Fry."

"Captain Fry," Val repeated. "Never heard of him. You selling me a bag of shit?"

"No! No, never, I'd never—he's a military man. Got drummed out but makes us all still call him captain. Lives over yonder."

"Give yonder a name."

"Fort Worth! He lives in Fort Worth, over off Granbury Road, near the river! Big old place. A real palace. He has—" There was that stutter again, like his eyes were blinking without his lids moving at all. "He has parties."

"What kind of parties?"

The man shrugged. "Just parties." That was a lie, but Val thought Rollins would rather swallow his tongue than to go on. "Fry brought the kid. Fry took her away. That's all I know, mister. Swear to God."

"Don't swear to God. Swear to me."

"I swear!"

"Get out."

"What?"

"Get out. I want you to run and keep on running."

"Mister, this is my house!"

"Pigs wouldn't claim it as a sty. Get out." Val stepped back and made a small *go* gesture with the gun. For a moment, Rollins just stared at him, then scrambled up out of the busted bed frame.

"What you gonna do?" he asked. He sounded meek now. Worried.

"Burn it down," Val said. "Trust me. You're better off with it gone. Plenty of old farmhouses around here sitting empty that you can squat in. Some got running water. A bath wouldn't hurt you."

There was something floating around in Rollins's alcohol-soaked brain, turning around and around; Val could see it. He didn't mean to burn the place down—at the very least, that would start a grass fire and burn those beautiful old live oaks—but on a hunch, he took out his lighter, shook it open, and flicked the wheel. At the sight of the flame, Rollins gulped.

"No, mister, don't you do that, you do that and it's on your head—"

"What is?" Rollins clammed up. Val stepped over to a tinder-dry pile of newspapers and filthy clothes. "What is?"

Rollins's hands shot out, and he said, "No!" He rushed past Val, kicked the clothes out of the way, and underneath, lo and behold, there was a trap door. Under that, Val expected to see some precious stash of bills, maybe, or a few undrunk bottles of rotgut.

It was a little girl.

It was Marion.

He blinked, looked at Rollins, who looked back. His eyes reflected the orange of the lighter flame like hell's own lanterns, but he said, "Maybe a reward, ain't there?"

Val came damn near to putting a bullet in him right then, because the word *reward* rang in his head with the terror in the girl's open eyes, the filthy state of her down in that hole, the dirt-smudged cast on her arm. Without taking his eyes off Rollins, he crouched down and offered Marion a hand. "Come on, baby," he said. "It's all right. You're safe now."

She cringed. He didn't blame her. God only knew what kind of fear a white man put in her at the moment.

"Rollins. You've got five minutes to get a head start, and then I'm heading for the cops. They're going to hunt you down like a rabid dog."

"I didn't *do* nothing!" Rollins insisted, almost tearfully, but it was half angry now. He glared at the kid. "I coulda let her burn you know! Woulda been *your fault*!"

And if Val hadn't threatened that, and Rollins hadn't been scared of a murder rap ... he'd come so close to believing Rollins and chasing after Fry, and Marion would have been right there, abandoned.

What would Rollins have done then? Only one answer for someone like Rollins: Get rid of the evidence. Maybe he'd have gone the coward's way, just left her there to die of hunger and thirst. Maybe when Val realized his mistake, he'd come back to find this little girl, this living little girl, a mummified corpse like Tilde.

"Run," Val told him. He almost wished Rollins wouldn't, but the scarecrow took to his heels, busting out the open door into the shadows of the live oaks, running for his life.

Val put the lighter down and holstered the gun. Then he reached down into the hole and picked up the child. She was trembling, but not crying, not at all. Her eyes were wide and dry, and she stared at him with a bottomless dread. Her arms hung limp at her sides. Alive, though. He could feel the too-fast beating of her heart.

Alive.

He felt a sudden pressure behind his eyes and blinked the tears away and there, in the doorway, stood Tilde.

She was smiling at him warmly. "Thank you, Val," she said. "Sorry I couldn't tell you. Rules are rules. Don't have to like them, but I have to follow them. So do you."

"Tilde—" He looked down at her niece in his arms, a slight, feverish weight. "This isn't all of it, is it?"

"All of it?" Tilde's laugh had a dark red edge of sadness and anger to it. "Val. It ain't even the *beginning* of it."

Marion, Missing

CHAPTER 7

He took Marion straight to the Fort Worth cops, skipping Arlington because it was a six-man operation that wouldn't give a shit about a little Negro girl found out in some shack. At least the big city cops had a missing persons report, even if they hadn't gone out of their way to look into it.

He used the pay phone to call Mr. and Mrs. Carlyle, and waited with Marion until they got to the police station downtown. He let them take care of calling the girl's parents.

Then he gave his statement and a full description of Rollins and where to find the tarpaper shack, and for good measure, threw the Arlington clinic quack under the wheels, too. Bastard probably had a fancy house and pool off the backs of the people he swindled.

When he gave her back to her grandparents, she latched on to her grandmother instantly, burying her face in the woman's shapeless coat while Mrs. Carlyle, tears streaming down her face, murmured comforts and stroked her hair.

Old man Carlyle took Val's hand and gravely shook it. He was crying too, but in a way that was harder to notice. "You're a good man," he said. "A good man. Our Matilde was right. I'm ashamed to say we didn't cotton to her sharing time with someone like you, but you're a do-right man."

Not really, Val wanted to tell him. He didn't. Better to let people believe what they wanted.

He wished, though, that little Marion had clung to him just a little. Drawn a little comfort from him.

"Don't fret," Tilde said in his ear. He turned away from the happy little family, and there she was, standing right beside him. She stared at her aunt and uncle with a calm expression, but there was a little regret there, too. A little sadness. "She'll be all right now. You got her before the worst could happen."

"Before she went back to Fry," he said, but in a whisper, in case people started noticing he was talking to himself in the middle of the detective bullpen. "You said there was more."

"There's more," Tilde agreed. "If you're up to it, Val. Are you?"

"Ain't I always?" It was a bitter little question, and she smiled in response, his ghost, his muse, his Tilde. He'd been half in love with her, and she'd known it, but beyond a couple of drinks and a dance or two in private, they'd been strictly business.

Tilde's choice. *Men can't work with women they sleep with,* she'd told him, which might be true and might not, but she thought it was. On the whole, he'd liked having her around enough that having her in his bed for a night or two didn't seem like a good enough tradeoff. That, he could get cheap dates all over town.

It wasn't just her smile, or the way she looked at him, like she knew him and liked him anyway. It wasn't just the way she looked or smelled or even the snappy, zinging power of her mind. It was just ... Tilde. The package. And maybe in another time ...

He shut it down, then, because it wasn't another time. It was *this* time, and he had work to do.

Captain Fry. If Rollins hadn't just desperately thrown out some useless bait, there was something there, something juicy, and a trail that needed following.

Fry had taken Marion.

Val needed to know why.

He put on his hat, nodded to the detective who'd taken his statement, and left.

CHAPTER 8

According to the phone book, Cornelius Fry lived out in a tony section of Fort Worth reserved for mansions and those who could afford them. Nice drive, unlike the weedy roads out to Rollins's place. These were paved two-lane roads, winding along smoothly past stately trees and careful gardens bursting with flowers, even in this heat. The lawns were velvet green and trimmed within an inch of their lives, and must have taken half the Trinity River to water through this long summer drought.

He found the address easily enough. It had little miniature castle towers holding iron gates across the driveway, and there was a man on duty in one of them in a muddy blue uniform—not police, private security. Carrying a respectable gun on his hip, though. With his hat on, he looked almost like somebody with real power, and he crossed to lean in Val's window to say, "Help you, sir?"

"I'm looking for Captain Fry," he said. "Cornelius Fry."

"I'm sorry, Captain Fry doesn't take visitors without prior appointments." The guard touched the brim of his hat. "Nice day to you, sir."

It was a full-power blow-off, and Val's rusty old Chrysler failed to impress. He pulled out his credentials and flashed them. "I think he'll see me," he said. "Just tell him I have some questions for him."

The guard didn't blink. "That's a private investigator's card, not police," he said. "So I'm asking you nicely to turn your car around and go."

Damn. He had to run into somebody sooner or later who actually looked, but this wasn't the moment he'd wanted the dice to fail him. "Here's my card," he said. "Tell him to call me."

He handed over the rectangle and watched the guard put it in his pocket, then put the Chrysler into reverse, turned, and drove away.

Not that far, though. He found a public park that overlooked the Trinity and pulled in under some trees—partly to cut the heat, and partly so that, when he looked over at Tilde, he wouldn't see that unearthly shimmer under her skin, or the blood.

"So I don't know what this is," he said. "Maybe I have a tumor on my brain. Maybe you're an angel. Maybe you've come right out of hell itself; I don't know. I just want to know what you want me to do here. Why do you care, Tilde?"

For answer, she pointed into the back seat, where he'd piled up all the boxes with their old cases. On top lay the folder marked with the name SANDS, MATILDE. Inside it was all the stuff he didn't want to read, and couldn't stop seeing every time he closed his eyes. Tilde's body, photographed in shimmering black and white like some modern art piece. The dry, clumsily typed account by the detective of how she'd died that sapped every drop of humanity from the event. Somebody had spilled coffee on part of the notes. The whole file smelled of it, old, stale beans, damp paper, frustration.

Tilde picked it up and dropped it in his lap.

No. Tilde was a ghost, a phantom, a figment of his own imagination. She couldn't pick something up.

But he felt the file hit his legs, and it was in that moment that he accepted the impossible thing.

Tilde was dead.

Tilde was in the car with him.

The sensation swept over him like red-hot pins and needles, and the file folder in his lap—olive drab, leftover army surplus he'd gotten for peanuts—swam and rippled as he stared at it, like the car had filled up with water when he wasn't looking. He shut his eyes and breathed in, out, deeper and deeper, trying to keep himself from drowning.

Tilde was in the car with him. Really here.

"Val," she said, and it was her voice, the low, sweet rasp of it as familiar to him as the worn wood of the partner's desk, or the tap of her heels on the floor. "Don't you go soft on me, now. You've never been soft."

No, that was true. He was a lot of things—rough around the edges, thick as a brick—but he'd never been some swooner. "You're really here," he said. He half wanted her to laugh and tell him he was crazy.

"Yes," she said. "I am. For now, anyway. I can't always stay."

"Why?"

"Reasons."

"That doesn't cut it, Tilde. Whose reasons?"

"Not mine, not yours. That's all I can tell you about it." She paused, and looked away. "I always thought you were a hell of a man, Warren. I thought maybe someday we'd—" She waved it away like an annoying fly. "Someday. Worst word anybody ever invented."

"Next to should've," he said. "I should've danced with you more. I should've danced you right into that hotel room. I should've married you, Tilde."

"Married?" She turned back to him, and her eyes were so beautiful he almost forgot she was dead. Almost. "Don't be a fool. I don't think you understand how hard it is for a Negro woman to be free in this world ... free of her parents, free of men, just *free* to be a person in her own right. It's like we were born with all the burden of our people, and then all the burden of Eve piled on top of it. I wasn't ever going to marry—not you, not anybody. That was *my* freedom."

He knew that. He knew how much she'd wanted to be on her own, be independent and fierce and not turn to him for much. And it made him angry enough to say, "Goddammit, why did you go off on your own and get killed? What kind of freedom is *that*?"

"Same kind you got," she said, ice to his fire. "If you went and got shot today, people would say you were a brave man, you died trying to save that little girl. You died a hero. With men, it's always about what you were *doing*. With women, it's different. It's never about what we did. That's what I hate about the world, Val. It always tries to make brave women look like they got some comeuppance for not minding their place. *I died trying to save lives.* I'm not ashamed of that."

She'd shamed him. He'd never thought of it like that, of how he'd said about women sometimes, *damn fool shouldn't have been there, she practically asked for it.* They all said it, like women had a place they were *supposed* to be, like they had lines they shouldn't cross. Tilde was right. He'd always looked at the freedom of women as different.

"Death's just the cost of doing the business we do," she told him. "We're dancing with the devil here. Both of us know that."

Dancing with the devil. He remembered the rank little shack, the blank horror of Marion's eyes. He'd done his job; he'd put her back in the arms of her family. But he knew there was more. Rollins wasn't smart enough or brave enough to have killed anyone. Especially not Tilde.

"Are you ready?" she asked him. The sun was starting to go down, firing harsh lines of orange across the sky like distress flares. It went down fast, here. You could see it sinking. "You can say no, Val."

"If I do, will you still talk to me?"

Tilde didn't smile. Didn't blink. She said, "No. Never again."

Val pulled in a deep breath, opened up the file, and began to read.

CHAPTER 9

Twenty-seven pages later, he closed the folder and rested his head on the steering wheel like a man on the bad end of a three-day drunk. His heart was pounding. His mouth had the faint taste of bile.

Tilde was still sitting next to him with her hands folded neatly in her lap. There was a drop of dried blood on her skirt, and as he turned his head toward her, she restlessly picked at it.

"If you were killed by the bastard who killed these other women, then he saw you as a threat, pure and simple," he said. "You were his type, Tilde. You were the right age, the right race. But he killed you and dumped you without all the rituals. Like he was angry."

"I was a threat," she agreed. "I knew who he was."

"His name's not in the file," he said. "Why not?"

"Because he called me and told me to bring him everything with his name on it, or I'd never see Marion again," she said. She cocked her head. "He also told me not to tell anyone. I didn't. I knew you'd want to rush to the rescue and put your foot in it, and I couldn't risk that little girl's life. So I took him the pages about how I'd tracked him down, and I brought a gun."

"It wasn't with you."

"No." She smiled thinly. "Didn't do me any good. I didn't reckon on there being more than one to worry about. He had his driver cold-cock me from behind and take my gun, and then—"

Then it had been a frenzy of stabbing, and they'd shoved her behind the trash. Gone. Wouldn't have taken more than a minute, probably less.

He'd still been taking pictures of some soon-to-be divorced

man at a hot sheet motel when it had happened, and come back to find Tilde gone, with no note.

And trash men had found her. Days later.

"You said he had a driver. Rich men have drivers. Rich men like Fry."

"Rich, sick men have all kinds of people," she said. "People to watch their backs. People to cover up for them. People to look the other way. He's just killing colored women, and they don't think it's much of a loss. He'll keep on, Val. He won't stop 'til somebody stops him."

Sick bastard. Val closed his eyes again for a second, trying to shove the image away of Tilde dying, that maniac stabbing away. He'd never seen the man, but imagined him as hunched, rabbity, crazy-eyed fiend right out of silent movies.

"Then we stop him," he said. "Tilde—"

She was gone. He put his hand on the seat where she'd been and found it cool, cooler than it should have been in the heat.

He got out of the car, in the dying orange sunset, and opened up the trunk. He kept a shotgun back there, and a .38. He reloaded the .45 then checked both the other weapons to be sure they were loaded before he tucked the .38 behind his back and the shotgun under his arm. His shirt was sopping wet, but he was used to that now. The heat was never going to break.

It was never going to break him, either.

With the sky turning toward twilight, Val went across the park, toward the back walls of the fancy estates.

Toward Cornelius Fry.

CHAPTER 10

It wasn't as easy as all that.

He looked at the back wall of what he figured must have been Fry's estate, but it was twelve feet high, and on a slope, and there were no trees overhanging it, no convenient ladders lying around or ropes or even a solid branch. He wasn't getting in that easy.

The next wall down, though, looked much easier—just a little higher than his head, and with some decent protruding bricks for hand- and footholds. He swarmed up and dropped down on the other side, into the shaded corner of a very lovely expanse of green lawn dotted with tasteful islands of flowers and bushes. There was a little brook running in a stone culvert, meandering through and underneath a wooden pavilion in the center of the yard.

Nobody in sight. Not even a gardener. Val dusted off his hands and strolled along the wall, careful of the windows, but the big, blocky, three-story house was mostly dark. Where it wasn't, he saw a black woman dressed in a neat gray maid's uniform. She was ironing some clothes, and didn't look up.

The other end of the yard had another wall, but this one came equipped with a wooden gate surrounded by blooming lantana. Late afternoon bees buzzed, but they ignored him in favor of the pollen bounty. Just another lazy summer day in rich-people land, with a monster lurking next door.

He eased out and crouched down in the shadows between the wall and the house, getting the lay of things. These fancy digs might as well have been separate planets, he thought; they fenced each other out, planted tall, pointed cedars and hedges, and made it seem like they were alone in the world. This mansion had its own separate, large two-story garage over on the right, near the wall. Room for three cars, and servants' quarters over them that must have been larger than his own apartment, for sure.

He stared at the garage for a moment, then got up and moved fast into the leaning shadow of a cedar tree. The garage doors might make noise, too much of it if there were people upstairs, but there'd be ladders inside. Gardening supplies.

Val ducked back in the shadows as a large man came out a side door—Negro man in a suit, with a chauffeur's cap. He slid up one of the garage doors with a loud rattle and went inside, and Val heard a heavy, throaty engine start up.

The nose of a Rolls Royce eased out of the dark interior and drove out a few feet onto the crunchy gravel. It was glossy pearl white, that thing, with silver trim. Classy and excessive.

The chauffeur went in again and came out with a full, sloshing bucket and a sponge, and Val realized this was his chance. When the man turned his back and began slopping water onto the paint job, scrubbing off bug splashes and specks, he moved to the interior of the garage.

No ladders. How could there be no ladders? He'd expected at least four of them, neatly hung on the walls, but *nothing*. There must be a separate groundskeeper building, he realized, but that did him no good at all. Toting a twelve-foot ladder across the front of the house was sure to get him noticed, especially if one hand held a shotgun.

Val went out and around the side, and slipped in the door the chauffeur had first come out of. It opened on a narrow set of wooden stairs that were new enough not to creak, but he took time and care anyway. There were six rooms, all empty. Each bed neatly made, no dust, clean as an army barracks waiting for inspection. He found what he was looking for in the hall at the back—a trap door in the ceiling.

Attic access, with a pull-down ladder.

Val hurried up the narrow attic steps—no easy job, with the shotgun—and pulled the ladder up with a creak of hinges before he let the trap door spring shut again. It wasn't quite pitch black in here, thanks to a couple of dusty windows facing west, but near enough.

He picked his way through an antique's store stock of old furniture, scared himself with a reflection in an age-dotted old mirror, and found another window, half-blocked, on the side he needed. He wedged it open and leaned out.

It'd be a damn far jump into Fry's lawn on the other side, and he'd have to clear a forbidding iron fence topped with spear points—a KEEP OUT sign with teeth. No dogs that he could see, and no roaming security patrol. *I'm going to break my neck,* he thought.

Then he saw Tilde standing on the lawn, exactly where he'd need to land. She gestured to him.

All right, then. What the hell.

He pitched the shotgun first, and it hit the grass with a harmless *thump*. He took the .38 out and sent it flying, too. Last thing he needed was to crack his spine with it.

Then he took a deep breath, climbed up on the sill, holding to the brick with a hard, gritty grip, and stared at Tilde's upturned face.

He launched himself like a diver into a pool, tucked, and hit in a protective ball, then rolled on the soft grass and threw out his arms and legs to kill his momentum. It hurt like getting hit in the back with a sledgehammer, and he took a second to gulp in breath, but when he turned over on his side and climbed to his feet, everything still worked. Didn't *like* working, but tough. He'd hurt later.

After grabbing the .38 and shotgun, he moved for the shadows again. Fry's mansion was a good deal different than the grand old palace next door; this was more of a modern monstrosity, all angles and glass windows.

The lights were blazing less than twenty feet from him, and no curtains to obstruct the view. *Dammit.*

He tried to see a better way around, and as he did, he caught sight of the driveway. There were a good ten cars crowded in the semicircle, all high-end products, though not one had the quality of the Rolls next door. New money, not old. A bunch of drivers crouched nearby, rolling dice for pocket change. Whatever was going on, it was planning to last a while.

Parties, he remembered Rollins saying, and the strange flicker in his eyes. What kind of parties?

Tilde was next to him again; he knew without looking, because he smelled her floral perfume. There were no flowers in Fry's yard. Nothing but grass and a few trees that had been there when Indians roamed the place. Fry obviously wasn't one for garden strolls.

Val had no good choices. He got low and eased slowly toward the bright, floor-to-ceiling window glass, and risked a look inside.

It was a party, all right. A gathering of men, all in expensive suits, all the men pale and glossy with highballs in their fists. Laughing. Talking.

They had their backs to him. That seemed like a stroke of luck, and one he had to seize, so he rushed across the exposed ground, fast and low as a running coyote, and made it to the inky shadow beyond.

Then he looked back to see if anyone had spotted him. They hadn't. They were hooting and laughing. Music rattled the glass, and he recognized a hoochie coochie song, coming from a platter on a high-end record player that cost more than his Chrysler when it was new.

A Negro woman was stripping.

She stood on a hassock, wearing a spangly costume draped with gauzy veils, and as she bounced and swayed and turned, she pulled the veils and draped them teasingly over the men who watched. She looked like a professional, he thought. Somebody who knew her trade.

"Hurry," Tilde said, and he blinked and looked away. She was moving to the back of the house, past darker windowpanes. He was more careful. Hell, he wasn't dead yet, or invisible. He couldn't afford to forget that.

Toward the back of the place, the windows went away, replaced by smooth pale concrete that felt cool under his hands. Sunset was gone now, just a fading stain on the darkening sky. He turned the corner at the back ...

... and ran into a man in a chauffeur suit walking toward him. It was an old-timey costume, with jodhpur pants and high, shiny boots, and for a second, with Tilde standing there too, Val wondered if this wasn't some other ghost come up out of the night.

Then the man drew back a fist and slugged him, and that doubt was knocked right out of him. The guy had a hell of a right hook, and Val felt teeth crunch—cracked, maybe busted. The pain was an intense, red burst that exploded like a firework in his skull, and then disappeared in a monster roar of adrenaline that yelled at him to *kill the mug.*

He had the shotgun, but it was too loud for this. Ditto the other guns. This needed to be quiet, and that meant hard-knuckle fighting with a guy who clearly wasn't a virgin at it.

Wish I'd brought a knife, Val thought, and just as he did, the chauffeur obliged by pulling one. It was a buck knife, a wicked shiny thing with a curve and a hell of a point, and Val had a good, close look as it slashed toward him. He managed to jump back, and lost some coat to it, but the guy hadn't expected him to be that fast, and was off balance from the slash.

Val set his feet and rushed him, pinning the knife hand between them, and slammed the guy hard into the ground like a footballer on the gridiron, then planted a knee in the man's groin and leaned. He clamped a hand over the man's mouth to stifle a scream, and yanked the knife free.

Looked up at Tilde as he held the guy down.

She looked like an ice queen, lit by her own inner radiance. Never more like a ghost than that moment. He could see blood oozing from wounds, and making a slow red trickle down her jawline to drip on her white shirt. She said, "He's the one who coshed me at the train station."

Fry's driver. His accomplice. The one who'd dragged Tilde's body and thrown it away like trash to rot in the sun.

Val looked down into the man's wide eyes and said, "Fuck you," and stuck the knife in his heart, just like he'd been taught in the army. Clean and quiet. He twisted and felt the blade scrape bone, and the guy jerked two or three times, gulping against his hand, and then his body relaxed. Val rolled off before the bowels could let go. He looked down at himself. Apart from the ripped coat, he was his same disreputable self, except for a spray of blood he could hardly even see.

"One down," he said, and nudged the chauffeur with his foot. Just a body now, lifeless and empty. In the dark, it looked like he was lying down for a nap, except for the open eyes and the gaping mouth. "Hope you enjoy hell."

Tilde was already walking on, with purpose. He followed.

CHAPTER 11

At the far corner of the house, Tilde stopped, and hesitated. She looked, for the first time, uncertain. "Val," she said. "I never got out here. I don't know ... I don't know where she is."

"Where who is?"

"The girl," she said. "The one ... the next one. But she's here. Somewhere inside."

Tilde was telling him that she'd known where Fry lived, but not where he was keeping girls before he dumped them dead and used up. That was a letdown. "What about the dead being all-knowing? Isn't that what all those spiritualists say?"

"They lie," she said. "I'm not in heaven, Val. I'm not in hell, either. I'm in ... somewhere between. I can't always see what I want. Or tell you what you need. Rules, like I said."

"I know how much you hate rules."

"You said it, brother." Tilde smiled, and that made the dark knot inside of him let loose, just a little.

He knew he ought to feel something about knifing a guy, but he didn't. The brutal truth was, a man like that needed to be dead, and making him that way was justice. Rough justice, sure. He was willing to take the rap, if it came to it. For Tilde.

"You see a door around here?"

She pointed, and he saw a back door in the shadow of a sharp angled corner. No porch lights. Good. It was locked, but he jammed the knife in and put his weight on it, and the lock gave after two or three hard jerks. Lightweight stuff. Fry was too confident.

Beyond, the hall felt cool, and it was as dark as an inkpot. Val felt his way along the wall, and his fingers ran into a picture frame that scraped as it swayed. He froze and steadied it, then shut the door behind him with as much silence as he could muster. No telling who was in here.

From the front of the house, he heard a burst of laughter, hooting, catcalls, whistles. The stripper was down to brass tacks, he guessed. He wondered if she was going to go full service. Probably. Strippers didn't hike it all the way out here unless there was a good pot of money in it for them, and a lot of prossies stripped, too. Double the money. Probably less the fun.

At least they'd be occupied, whatever was going on. He felt along the wall again, avoiding the picture, and found a door. Closed, not locked, and as he eased it open he saw a rumpled bed and clothes on the floor. It wasn't a fancy enough bedroom for someone like Fry, so it must have been the chauffeur. Clearly, Fry didn't do barracks inspections and bounce quarters off of bedsheets.

The party in the living room was whooping it up. He didn't worry about noise now as he shut the door and walked down to the next room. Some kind of storage, full of junk. Rich man's junk—last year's radio model, statues, splashy modern art paintings leaning up against walls, rolled up priceless carpets.

In the corner, under a painting that looked like a splashes and smears of dried blood on a white canvas, there was a trap door inset in the smooth wood floor. He nearly missed it, poking around, and only saw it because Tilde shimmered into life standing on it, stared at him, and then melted into the blood painting.

As he moved the painting, he was struck by the smell. Didn't smell like paint. Any dick who'd been around a bloody crime scene knew that particular rotting stench; nothing stank like old blood.

He pulled back, stared at the thing, and looked at the artist's signature down in the corner.

Fry.

Son of a bitch.

He grabbed hold of the trap door handle and was about to

yank when he heard the tone of the party shift. Not wild gin-swilling jollity anymore. This had an ugly edge to it, and the lone female voice coming through had a stronger and stronger note of angry panic. "One at a time, fellas, I ain't a piece of meat—"

Then she screamed, and Val let go of the trap door and lunged for the door, racking the shotgun as he went.

Marion, Missing

CHAPTER 12

The stripper saw him first. She was naked, trying to crawl away, and her eyes were round as full moons, lit by desperation and fear. Men-shaped wolves in rich suits, pawing at her, howling.

Val saw stripes of blood on her back. Fingernails, a whip, he didn't know and didn't care. He skidded to a stop on the polished floor, aimed straight up with the shotgun, and fired into the lofty ceiling.

The boom froze everybody for a second, even the girl, and then he lowered the barrel to point it straight at the group of men and said, "Lady said no, fellas."

She scrambled not for him, but for her flimsy pile of discarded clothes; she jumped into the spangly briefs and top, left the shredded veils, and ran for it. Maybe one of those cars out there was hers, but he doubted it. He didn't doubt her will to run all the way to the protection of black streets. She'd make it.

"If you don't want to answer some cop questions, blow out of here," Val said to the men, who were still frozen, looking blank and shocked that somebody had put a stop to their good time. "Did you hear me? *Blow*!"

He racked the shotgun again, and that got feet beating the wood for the front door ... for everybody but one of them. Fry. He was a neat little man, fussy, in a charcoal gray suit tailored close, with an Errol Flynn pencil mustache and slick, military-short hair slicked into a black cap.

Red ascot instead of a tie. Pallid skin, blue shadows under his deep-set eyes. He was the kind of guy who'd smoke cigarettes in an ivory holder and wipe his hands after touching anyone who worked for a living.

The record had long since reached the end, and it just rotated mindlessly on the turntable, hissing out a steady, uneven rhythm.

As the last of the guests made it out the door, and the first of the jalopies out in the drive gunned it for freedom, Val took in the room. It was big, bigger than the cramped farmhouse he'd grown up in. Shimmering wood floor. Bear skin rug by the stark white brick fireplace, and a chrome bar in the corner stocked with more kinds of booze than the local package store. What furniture there was, was angled and uncomfortable and of that same eye-hurting white, with dots of red accents.

And then, there were the paintings, if you could call them that.

The one hanging over the fireplace was of a dead woman. Modern art these days was usually all angles and splashes, Val didn't get it, but this was more like Picasso, abstract but understandable. It was a woman lying on the bank of a river, dead-fish white, with something like a red scarf tied around her neck and blood splashed over her pallid skin.

Not Fry's work, though he recognized the others on the walls. Brownish-red splashes and smears on canvas.

His gallery of dead women.

Fry ignored Val, and the shotgun. He walked to the massive front door and closed it, locked it, and then went to the bar and poured himself a drink. Quite the expert at mixing a martini. He put two olives in it.

"You must be Valentine," Fry said. He had a light, clean, clear voice, nothing memorable, nothing like a cartoon villain's growl. Prep school diction, not a trace of a Texas accent muddying the pure vowels. "The partner." That sounded half amused. Fry finished concocting his martini and turned, leaning up against the bar as he sipped his drink. "You ruined my party."

"You ruined a lot of things." Val's voice was tight, but he had the anger under control. There was plenty of evidence here to seal this bastard's fate for the electric chair, and it would be better to watch him sizzle. Besides, the cops asked awkward questions—what Val was doing here, how he got in, the dead guy in the back. Questions he'd rather not have to ask with a shotgun abstract of a dead guy on the floor. Alive, Fry could answer questions. Dead, the cops might just put Val in the hot seat.

"That's one way of looking at it," Fry agreed calmly, and sipped his martini. He must have liked it, because he took another sip. "I saw you admiring the painting. Brilliant, isn't it?"

"Not the way I'd describe it."

"My sister," Fry said. "They found her on the banks of the Trinity when I was fourteen. She was eighteen, poor soul. My mother never got over it."

"You did though."

"Well, I coped." Fry's eyes, Val decided, were like opaque black windows, showing nothing at all. His smiles were rubbery and all surface. Whatever was underneath wore him like a fright mask. "One does, you know. Cope. I suppose you tracked your partner back to me somehow. She did come here to talk to me once. You can ask my chauffeur if you'd like. He can verify that she left quite safely."

"Tell me something," Val said. "I get your sister died— strangled and stabbed, I'm guessing. She was white. Why pick on colored women now?"

Fry sipped his martini, fished out a speared olive, and sucked it off with evident relish. "I don't understand your question, Mr. Valentine. Are you implying I have something to do with these poor, dead women?"

"What was going to happen to that chippie who just left?'

"Her?" Fry shrugged. "She'd do her job and get paid. Her job was to let us do what we wanted. Anything we wanted. Then she'd get paid and go home. Do you really think I kill women who come to my home, detective? What kind of monster do you think I am?"

"I don't know that we have a name for the kind of monster

you are," Val said. "But monster's good enough."

"Then shoot me," Fry said. "By all means, both barrels. Blow my chest into hamburger. The problem is, I'm a rich man. An important man, with friends. And you're a cheap, scrambling detective who slummed it with a Negro whore who got what she deserved."

"No," Tilde whispered in his ear. "Val. *Val.*" He needed that cool whisper just now, tamping down the fire erupting in his brain, trying to zip down his arm to his trigger finger. "Let him talk. You've got him. You've got him dead to rights. Call the cops."

Val spotted the fancy, sleek telephone on a side table—bright blood red, standing out against the white—and crossed to pick up the receiver.

Fry lost his insouciant smile. *Not so cocky now, you little shit.* His important friends, from the mayor on down, would defect and deny as fast as their fat little legs would carry them once evidence started piling up. Val cradled the receiver between his shoulder and ear, and reached down to rotate the dial for an operator. Didn't take his eyes off of Fry.

"*Val!*" Tilde's whisper was more of a scream this time, loud and urgent, but it was also too late. Something hit him in the back of the head, stunningly hard. Then, as he dropped the phone and tried to turn and bring the shotgun to bear, he got another blow, and felt something crack. Bone, for sure. Maybe his skull.

His fingers slipped off the shotgun, and he felt it spin away. He was off balance, and lurched into a pristine white leather chair. Red splashed on it, like Fry's ugly paintings, only this time he was the one painting with his own blood.

Somehow, he still had the phone's heavy weight gripped in his left hand, and he turned and swung wildly with it. He missed. The figure standing in front of him was wearing a tailored chauffeur's uniform, peaked cap, jodhpur pants, polished boots. *He's dead,* Val thought. *Jesus. Ghosts everywhere.*

But the driver wasn't a ghost. He wasn't the same person as

the dead man out back, either.

Fry had *two* drivers, and this one grabbed the red phone from Val's weakened grip, grinned nastily, and whipped it across Val's chin with stunning force. He felt a burst of white-hot pain, and then he was on the floor, drooling blood. When he looked up, Tilde was kneeling there right in front of him, bent over, looking desperate and anxious. The red flowers on her shirt were bleeding again. The hole in her head wept.

"Get up! Val, get up, you have to get up—"

She'd said it to herself, he thought, after she'd gotten cold-cocked at the train station. She'd come to and told herself to get up, but she hadn't managed it, and then Fry had taken out his sharp little icepick.

I have to get up, he told himself, and tried.

A polished boot to the head put him down in the dark.

Marion, Missing

CHAPTER 13

The room under the trap door was a storm shelter, solid concrete, fitted up with electric lights and big enough to offer tornado protection to half the neighborhood. It had conveniences—a soft leather armchair, for one, which sat in the corner, and what looked like a movie camera, with the lens winking at him from a tripod.

Val hung from a pair of chains attached to rings in the wall, and as he came awake—if you could call being this woozy *awake*—the sharp pain in his wrists was what really prodded him into alertness.

He got his wobbly knees firmed up, and that pain eased a little, but that just let the head throb for attention. He'd definitely gotten his skull cracked. Maybe bad enough to kill him, eventually. The pain was bad, the sick *wrong* feeling was worse.

Fry sat in the comfy leather chair in the corner, legs crossed, drinking a martini. Probably not the same one. Though it had two olives in it, again.

"Oh good," he said. "You're back. I didn't have a chance to properly introduce you to Gerald," he said. "We found Gerald's twin brother Alfred out back. Pity. They were very close—slept in the same bed, don't you know. I had to make Gerald leave until he calmed down. I'll let him come back in a little while. I'm sure you'll have a very good time together. You know, it's a pity I never had your Matilde as my guest down here. She'd have made such a pretty picture."

Val said nothing. He'd never thought he'd be grateful for the way Tilde died, but now ... now he was. Now he was happy she didn't have to die in front of that camera, and leave Fry art for his wall. He tested the chains. They were industrial strength, and would have held Hercules, much less some schmoe like him. He needed a key. Or a miracle. Both were just about as likely.

There was no vision of Tilde down here. The last he'd seen of her had been her on her knees, tell him to get up, desperation all over her face ... and she wasn't down here, to watch him die. He didn't blame her. He wouldn't be here either if he could've helped it.

"Thought you got your kicks with the girls," he said to Fry. "Not men."

"Meat is meat," Fry said, though he did look faintly put out by the reminder. "I won't be able to do *everything* to you, of course, but I feel that you should understand the process. Maybe we can make you female first. Or less male, at any rate. That would be something Gerald would enjoy."

Val swallowed a mouthful of blood and smiled. "He gets close enough to bite, I'll take some chunks," he said. "So which one of them hit Tilde on the skull? Alfie?"

"No, you killed the wrong twin, I'm afraid. That was Gerald. They alternate days."

"Too bad." Val stared at Fry's shadowy smile. "But you're the one who killed her."

"Guilty." Fry sipped the martini. "And once I've killed you as an appetizer, I'll move on to my main course."

Main course. Val blinked and looked around ... and saw the cage. It was made of steel bars, like something you'd keep a small, vicious animal in—too small for a human being, but somehow, the naked woman had been crammed inside in a ball. She was Negro, half-hidden by the shadows except where the lights shimmered on her smooth skin. He couldn't see her face.

Fry already had his next big, white canvas leaning up against the wall, with a little table loaded with paintbrushes.

"Thought the stripper was your next project," Val said. "You work fast."

"I always keep one in reserve, just in case. I've had a few slip the trap." Fry shrugged. "Doesn't matter. Nobody listens to them. I actually had one spirited little animal break free, get out to the road, and try to run away, and the police actually picked her up, can you imagine that? They brought her back to me to check her story. I told them she was a junkie prostitute, that I'd have my driver take her home. They just left her with me. I'm such an upstanding citizen, you know. I support the Fraternal Order of Police every fund drive." Fry's eyes gleamed suddenly. "She was my best work. Two weeks, I kept her."

Val wanted to vomit, but he figured that would offend no one but him. "How long you figure on keeping me?"

"I don't," Fry said, and put the martini aside on a fussy little cocktail table. He stood up, removed his charcoal-colored coat, and rolled up his crisp white sleeves as he studied Val like a live art model. "I killed your partner with an ice pick to the heart. Fast and efficient. The other strikes were just—entertainment. Especially the one to her brain. I wanted to know how it felt, but it was disappointing. No real resistance to it, you know? Like stabbing a particularly thick tub of jelly. One day I need to experiment more with that."

He reached down and unbuckled Val's belt, which made Val's skin shiver into goose pimples all over. *Shit.* "Tell me," Val said, and tried to make it sound calm and conversational. "Did you kill your sister, or do you just get hard thinking about it?"

That made Fry stop and look him straight in the eyes. The man had black, soulless eyes, like nothing Val had ever seen before. He'd looked into the eyes of killers, of men *trying* to kill him in the war, and he'd never seen anything like this. There was something deeply empty in there.

"Why, both, actually," Fry said. "I don't think I ever told anyone that before. Kudos, Mr. Valentine, you really are a good detective."

"Not good enough," Val said, and meant it. "If I had been, I'd have backed up my partner. I'd have tracked you down. Tilde would be alive, and you'd be a head hanging on my office wall."

"Well," Fry said, "I never said you were a *great* detective." He unbuttoned Val's pants, and they slid down to pool around Val's ankles. "Don't worry, I'm not attracted to you," he said. "Far from it. I just want you free of all these clothes. They get in the way, you see, and—"

From upstairs, there was the sound of a doorbell. It was coming through a speaker, set in the wall. *Doorbell.*

Fry took a step back from him, staring at the speaker set into the wall, and pressed a button underneath it. "Gerald? Answer it."

"Yes, boss," said a low, gravely voice.

"Leave the speaker on. I want to hear."

"Yes, boss."

"Maybe it's the cops," Val said. "The stripper got away. Maybe this time, they're not going to dismiss it. Maybe this time, they'll want to come inside and check out your house, find your little horror show. What do you think, Fry? Feeling lucky?"

"I'm always lucky," Fry said absently. He moved closer to the speaker.

Val heard the door unlocking, and the sound of crickets chirping, and then a soft old Negro voice said, "Mister Fry, sir?"

"Mr. Fry's not here," Gerald said. "Beat it. We got no jobs here."

"Sir, I ain't here about a job," said that soft voice. It sounded familiar. "I'm here about Matilde Sands."

Jesus God. He did know that voice. It had been in his office what seemed a lifetime ago now, but had just been this morning, somehow. A shapeless woman in a coat. *Jesus, no. No.*

"Tilde sends her love," Mrs. Carlyle said, and there was a *bang* loud enough to rattle the speaker, echo around the concrete room, and then another *bang,* and another one, and a loud, scraping thump.

Footsteps. Calm footsteps. Heels on wood.

"Basement!" Val yelled. He didn't know if she could hear him over that speaker, or if it was set to one-way, but it was worth a shot.

Fry bared his teeth and turned those burning, black eyes on him. He snatched up something from the table, an ice pick, and rushed at him. He'd kill Val, then take the old lady, and nothing would change. *Nothing.*

Val heaved his legs up and wrapped them around Fry's neck, trapping the man's chin between his thighs and squeezing hard. He felt hot, agonizing stabs as Fry flailed at him with the icepick, trying for something vital but too panicked to hit anything on target.

He squeezed tighter. Tighter. Then he jerked himself up, putting his full weight hard on the cuffs, wrapping his hands around the chains and lifting Fry off his feet using the muscles of his back and stomach. Even then, it was barely enough— barely an inch of air between Fry's frantically scrabbling shoes and the concrete floor.

It was enough.

Hold on, he told himself, because Tilde wasn't there to tell him. *Hold on. Hold on. Hold on hold hold hold hold.*

Fry landed more stabs to back of his thighs and buttocks and the sides of his hips. Blood streamed to the floor, but Val kept himself locked there, a human gallows, and the stabs got weaker, shallower, and then the icepick dropped and rolled away, and Fry was slapping at him with ineffectual little pats.

Then he was entirely limp. His face was an ugly reddish purple, his tongue protruding, crimson eyes bulging. There was blood coming from his nose.

Val held on. He wasn't sure he knew how to let go anymore.

He heard the trap door swing up, and the tap of heels on the wood, and saw Mrs. Carlyle—and behind her, Mr. Carlyle. Both of them had snub-nosed revolvers, blue steel. Mr. Carlyle was still wearing his fedora, and Mrs. Carlyle that same old coat. She faltered when she saw him, and finally, finally, he felt like he could let go.

Fry hit the floor like a sack of wet meat, spattering blood from the puddle beneath Val's legs. He looked small down there. Val lowered his legs and took his weight on his feet again—tried, anyway. He couldn't manage. Everything was strange and watery and bloody.

Mrs. Carlyle was talking to him, touching his face. Mr. Carlyle was searching Fry's pockets, and he came up with a key and unlocked one of Val's cuffs, then the other. Val slid down the wall. He'd stopped feeling the pain now. He just felt numb. His legs were a mess.

"Give me a gun," he whispered hoarsely. Mrs. Carlyle exchanged a look with her husband, and handed hers over. Val put the barrel to Fry's temple and pulled the trigger. Brains and blood exploded, more modern art for Fry's wall. Some of it actually landed on blank canvas. "Both of you, get out of here. Get. You were never here."

"We can't leave you," Mr. Carlyle said. "You need help, Mr. Valentine."

He looked at the old man and said, "How'd you get here, anyway?"

"I believe in spirits," Mrs. Carlyle said. She leaned forward and kissed him on the forehead. He felt tears run wet down his face—his, hers, didn't matter. "And I listen when they talk to me."

Carlyle opened up the cage and helped the girl crawl out of it. He took Fry's bloody charcoal-colored coat and draped it around her like a cape; she could barely walk, and she had the same empty, terror-filled look that Val had seen in Marion's eyes.

He wondered what his own eyes looked like, just now. How they'd looked to Fry as he was choking to death and staring into them.

"Get her out of here," Val said hoarsely. "There's plenty of evidence. Just go."

They did. He was left sitting on the bloody concrete floor with a dead monster, and it took him half an hour to summon up the strength to crawl up the stairs, find the red phone, and call the cops.

He took a certain savage satisfaction in bleeding all over the clean wood floor.

Marion, Missing

CHAPTER 14

When he woke up in the hospital, he was handcuffed to the bed. Funny. Under that, he had bandages around his wrists from where he'd cut them up against the cuffs, and bandages around his head, and over the lower half of his body. Didn't hurt much, though. He felt light and buzzy, like somebody had pumped him full of sunshine.

A nurse in a starched white hat leaned over him and smiled. "You're awake," she said. "Hello."

"Where am I?"

"St. Joseph's," she said. Funny, he'd been here before, looking for Marion, down in the Negro ward in the basement. This was upper floors; he could see downtown Fort Worth from his window. The soft light said it was still early morning. "Take it easy, sir, you've got a skull fracture and a lot of damage to your lower body, including several stabs to your kidneys. You've had surgery to repair the damage."

Well, that sounded good. He didn't think he was dying, but then again, after the day he'd had, dying might feel this good.

"Fry?"

She looked puzzled. "Sir?"

"Is Fry dead?" She still looked vacant, and it didn't matter, now he remembered. He'd stuck the snub-nose against the man's discolored face and made damn sure of it. Brains on the canvas. Almost funny. Almost. "Never mind." He rattled the cuffs. "Cops?"

"They wanted to make sure you didn't try to leave without making a statement," she said. "You're not under arrest or anything. They said you were a hero."

He wasn't. That was for damn sure. But he let her think it, because he was just too tired to care, and his eyelids felt heavy as concrete.

When he opened them again doctors were poking and prodding, and a flat-nosed detective sat in the chair next to his bed reading a newspaper. The headline was about the stock market, not Fry. Too bad.

"Valentine," the cop said, and folded the paper and leaned forward. "Hell of a thing. I'm Jansen. Homicide."

"Seems about right," Val said. "Seeing as how there were a whole lot of dead women."

Jansen said nothing.

"You been in the house?"

"I have."

"Every one of those paintings—"

"Blood," Jansen said. "We counted twelve in total, not including the one with his brains on it you painted. We're looking at closed cases now, and unsolveds. Going to be a hell of a mess, you know. Innocent men convicted. The newspapers are going to lap it up like cream. Police misconduct. Ineptitude, if they can spell that."

"Surprised you can."

Jensen smiled thinly. He was a middle-aged guy, tough, with the scarred eyebrows of a boxer. One of his ears looked lopsided. "On a good day. How'd you get onto Fry?"

"My partner," Val said. "Matilde Sands. She was onto him. He snatched her niece to get her alone, and he killed her. So that's another one. No painting for her, though. Just a grave."

Jansen made a note in his little black book and nodded. "Yeah, I saw where you brought the little girl back. You know how that looks, right?"

Val blinked. "What?"

"In a day, you found this missing kid and brought her home, then end up with a three dead guys—*three*—at the estate of one of the richest men in Fort Worth. Smart money's trying to say you were in on the whole thing. An accomplice, maybe. Maybe you ice-picked your partner when she found out."

Val shut his eyes. "That's the smart money? Sounds dumb to me."

"Yeah, the smart money's bought and paid for by Fry's pals, we know that. Just relax while we work out all the kinks."

"Where am I gonna go?"

Jensen gave him another long look. "I know you're a do-right guy, Valentine. But let us work the angles."

"You did such a good job with all the other patsies you put away."

"And we're getting them out. You won't see the inside of a jail. Promise." Jansen hesitated, and cleared his throat. "Doc talk to you?"

Had he? Val couldn't remember, really. There'd been some man in a coat, thick dark hair and a baritone voice that boomed too loud, something about survival rates and chances. He hadn't caught it all.

"That skull fracture's pretty bad, they say," Jensen said. "Hope it works out. I know the odds aren't good, so ... good luck, Valentine."

"Yeah."

Jensen clicked his pen and put away his notebook, and leaned forward on his elbows. "Everything checks out about this, you come out a hell of a hero," he said. "Hope you live to see that."

Then he was gone. He'd left the paper. Val pulled it over and turned it, one-handed. He found word of Fry's death on page four, a skinny little two-column story.

Millionaire and two servants found dead. Nothing about the rest of it. *Suspicious circumstances.* He imagined there'd be a lot of pearl-clutching behind the gates of the neighborhood tonight, and a run on armed security patrols to keep the imaginary marauders from the richly paneled doors.

When this story broke, it'd be bloody.

He slept again, and woke at night, to more nurses taking fluids and making him pee in bedpans. He felt woozy and slippery. Once they were gone, they dimmed the lights a little, and he stared out at the glittering Fort Worth skyline. It all looked far away.

"Hey, sailor," Tilde said. She was sitting in the chair next to him, legs crossed. This time, her white sweater was pristine, and the side of her head perfect. Her skin looked rich and healthy. "How you feeling?"

"I was army, not navy."

"Figure of speech," she said, and leaned forward. He got lost in her eyes. Living or dead, she was more beautiful than he'd ever realized. "Don't worry about Fry. The cops know what happened. They're finding so much evidence even money can't cover it all up. Besides, nobody's there to inherit. The governor's itching to get his hands on it for the state."

She was shimmering in the air—no, the whole room was shimmering. He felt so tired. "Your people okay?"

"They will be," she said. "I didn't know what else to do, Val. I had to help you. I couldn't just ..."

"Let me die? The way I let you die?" His throat felt tight now, and his eyes stung. He turned away from her luminous smile. "I was a petty bastard. Didn't want to back you up on the case. You had reason not to trust me. You know I never saw Negro cases as something worth taking. I was wrong about that. A real bastard."

"Doesn't matter now," she said.

He felt the stroke of her fingers on his cheek, cool but not cold anymore. Real as anything.

"You found Marion. You saved the girl down in that cellar. You saved all the girls who would have ended up down there, too."

"That doesn't make me good."

"Makes you somewhat less than bad. Face it. You'll just have to put up with being a good man after all." She leaned closer, and when he turned and met her eyes, he saw the look in hers. The look he never recognized before, the warm, sweet, simple feeling. Normal as heartbeats. "I love you, Warren Valentine."

"Jesus," he whispered. "I love you, Tilde. Don't go."

"I won't," she said, and leaned forward to kiss him. He could feel her lips on his, there and not there, sweet and cool and everything he'd ever wanted. "I won't ever leave you again."

He felt something shift in his head: bone, some blood vessel blowing. Whatever it was, it was bad. Didn't matter. He was going sweetly, slowly quiet now.

Not so bad.

He was with her. He'd always be with her.

And that was all he wanted.

The End

Did you enjoy *Marion, Missing*?

For more information, and to keep up with her release news and other updates, please visit Rachel's website:
http://www.rachelcaine.com

Check out the rest of Rachel's books at….

Amazon: http://www.amazon.com/Rachel-Caine/e/B001ILHJEA

B&N: http://www.barnesandnoble.com/s/rachel-caine

iBooks: https://itunes.apple.com/us/author/rachel-caine/id316654014?mt=11

Kobo:
https://store.kobobooks.com/search?Query=Rachel+Caine

About The Author

Rachel Caine is the New York Times, USA Today, and #1 internationally bestselling author of more than 45 novels and more than 100 short stories.

Novels:
(as Roxanne Longstreet)
Stormriders
The Undead
Red Angel
Cold Kiss
Slow Burn

(as Roxanne Conrad)
Copper Moon
Bridge of Shadows
Exile, Texas

(as Julie Fortune)
Stargate SG-1: Sacrifice Moon

(as Bridgette Luna)
Unfiltered & Unsaved

(as Rachel Caine)
The Weather Warden series
Ill Wind
Heat Stroke
Chill Factor
Windfall
Firestorm
Thin Air
Gale Force
Cape Storm
Total Eclipse

The Outcast Season series
Undone
Unknown
Unseen
Unbroken

The Red Letter Days series
Devil's Bargain
Devil's Due

The Athena Force shared world series
Athena Force: Line of Sight

The Revivalist series
Working Stiff
Two Weeks' Notice
Terminated
The Morganville Vampires series
Glass Houses
The Dead Girls' Dance
Midnight Alley
Feast of Fools
Lord of Misrule
Carpe Corpus
Fade Out
Kiss of Death
Ghost Town
Bite Club
Last Breath
Black Dawn
Bitter Blood
Fall of Night
Daylighters
Midnight Bites
Prince of Shadows

The Great Library series
Ink and Bone
Paper and Fire

www.ingramcontent.com/pod-product-compliance
Lightning Source LLC
Chambersburg PA
CBHW020549130626
46552CB00007B/2821